WEST SLOPE COMMUNITY LIBRARY
(503) 292-6416
MEMBER OF
WASHINGTON COUNTY COOPERATIVE
LIBRARY SERVICES

Nathan's Fishing Trip

by Lulu Delacre

SCHOLASTIC INC./New York

WEST SLOPE COMMUNITY LIBRARY
3670 S.W. 78th
PORTLAND, OREGON 97226

For Phyllis,
who taught me the meaning of the word perfect,
and Béatrice Hélène,
my niece and godchild

A LUCAS • EVANS BOOK

Copyright © 1988 by Lulu Delacre.
All rights reserved. Published by Scholastic Inc.
SCHOLASTIC HARDCOVER is a registered trademark of Scholastic Inc.

No part of this publication may be reproduced in whole or in part,
or stored in a retrieval system, or transmitted in any form or by any
means, electronic, mechanical, photocopying, recording, or
otherwise, without written permission of the publisher. For
information regarding permission, write to Scholastic Inc.,
730 Broadway, New York, NY 10003.

Library of Congress Cataloging-in-Publication Data
Delacre, Lulu.
Nathan's fishing trip.

Summary: Nicholas Alexander takes Nathan on his first fishing trip,
but after great difficulty in catching a trout, they haven't got the
heart to eat it.
1. Fishing—Fiction. 2. Elephants—Fiction.
3. Mice—Fiction. I. Title.
PZ7.D3696Nat 1988 [E] 87-12454
ISBN 0-590-41281-7

12 11 10 9 8 7 6 5 4 3 2 1   8 9/8 0 1 2 3/9

Printed in the U.S.A.   23

First Scholastic printing, March 1988

It was sunrise...

Nathan was packing the sandwiches
as Nicholas Alexander untied the boat.
Now they were set, ready to go.

Very, very early they had gathered
everything needed for
Nathan's first fishing trip:
two fishing rods,
hooks,
lures,
and flies;
a bucket for the fish,
and the worms, of course,
the worms.

The boat softly crossed the waters
to the rhythm of the motor's sound—
brrrrrrrrmmnn—
All of a sudden Nicholas stopped.
"This is a good place
to start your fishing lessons," he said.

"Sir, first you tie
the hook to the line.
Then you throw it
into the lake. You sit
very still and wait.
Just wait."

"Can't I hold it yet?"
asked Nathan. "Please?"
"Well...fine,
but sit in the center
and be still."

"Something bit!
Something bit!"
cried Nathan.

"Hold the line tight
and take it in slowly!"
exclaimed Nicholas.
"Oh! Oh! Oh!"
Nathan shouted.

"It swam away...

with my fishing rod!" cried Nathan.
"It is quite all right, sir,
we still have another rod
and enough lures and hooks
to make a good catch," said Nicholas.
"Just wait. You'll see."

Three hooks, five flies
and seven lures later,
Nicholas declared
they had to try something better.

"Yes," he said, "I think
the fish around here must like
nice, fat, tasty
garden worms."

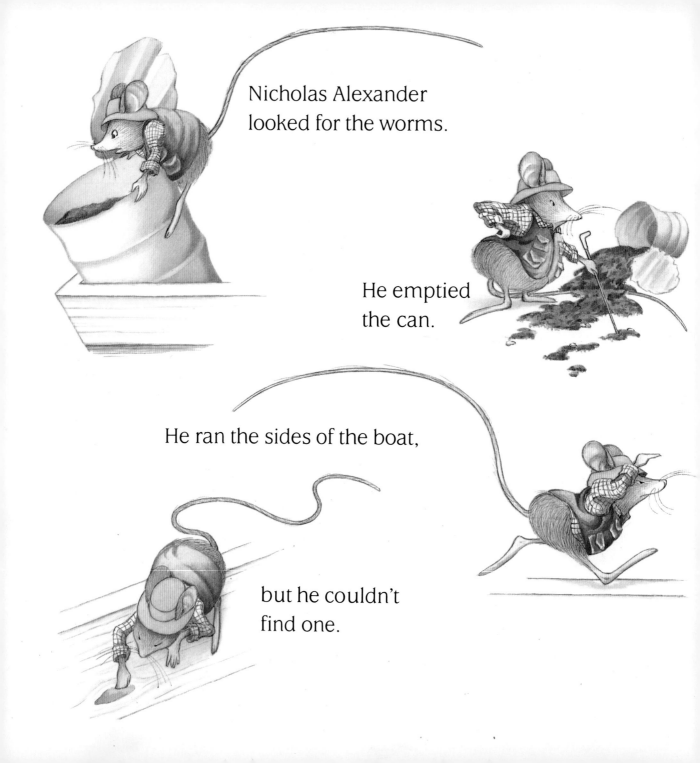

Nicholas Alexander
looked for the worms.

He emptied
the can.

He ran the sides of the boat,

but he couldn't
find one.

He sniffed and searched for the worms.

They looked all around
until, at last, they found a hole in the lunchbag.

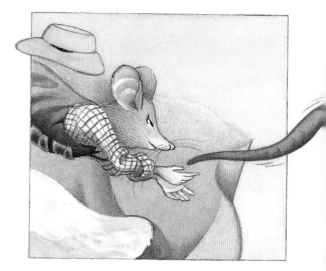

A fat, little worm
was nibbling inside.

Nicholas threw himself
on top of it,
but it squirmed away.

Then Nathan threw himself on top of it—

"Grabbed it!" cried
Nicholas Alexander.

They straightened the boat
and recovered everything...
but the rod.

"I told you to sit still!" exclaimed Nicholas.

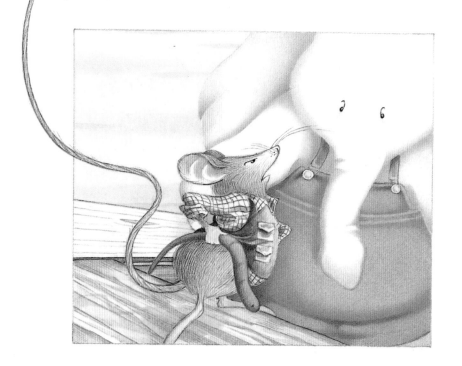

"It's going to be quite impossible
to fish a trout without a fishing pole.
We might as well
forget the whole affair."

"I've got an idea!" cried Nathan.
He took the worm with his trunk
and plunged his head into the water.

A few minutes later
he emerged beaming, proudly
holding a beautiful rainbow trout.
"It's magnificent!" exclaimed Nicholas.
"Congratulations, my friend!
Quick, put it in the bucket.
I can't wait to roast
and taste it!"

Tired but happy
they steered toward land
and docked the boat.
They built a nice warm fire
and prepared everything
for a late, well-deserved meal.

The trout was still bouncing
and struggling inside the bucket.
"This one is going to be
quite delicious, moist and tender
and sprinkled with lemon,"
Nicholas said, licking his whiskers.

Nathan peeked inside.
He watched the trout for a while.
"It's such a pretty fish," he thought.
His face saddened.
"Do we really have to eat it?"
he asked.

Nicholas looked at Nathan.
Then he looked at the trout—

He tilted the bucket toward the lake
and, as the trout swam away, he said,
"No, sir, I think
we can be quite content
with peanut butter
and cucumber sandwiches."

8/97

E
DEL

WEST SLOPE COMMUNITY LIBRARY
3670 S.W. 78th
PORTLAND, OREGON 97226